This igloo book belongs to:

....

igloobooks

Published in 2017
by Igloo Books Ltd
Cottage Farm
Sywell
NN6 0BJ
www.igloobooks.com

STA002 0617
6 8 10 11 9 7
ISBN: 978-1-78197-295-3

Printed and manufactured in China

The Magical
Fairy Ball

igloobooks

All of Fairyland was in a flutter. The Fairy Queen's new palace was almost finished and she was throwing a magnificent palace-warming ball to show it off. Everyone in the kingdom was invited. That morning, a beautiful handwritten invitation had magically appeared on each little fairy's pillow. Honesty, the detective fairy, was so excited that she rushed straight over to show hers to her best friend Harmony.

Harmony, who was the peace fairy, was busy as usual. Honesty waited patiently as she settled an argument two frogs were having over a lily pad. Then she waved the royal invitation under her friend's nose and demanded to see hers. "I haven't got one," whispered Harmony. "I haven't been invited."

"But you must have received an invitation," said Honesty. "I'm going to look under your pillow. It might have slipped out of sight." Honesty's nose began to twitch, just as it always did when she felt some detective work coming on. She searched high and low but she couldn't find the invitation anywhere. "It must have gotten lost in the fairymail," she decided at last.

Harmony shrugged her shoulders and tried to smile. "I expect the Queen forgot to send me one. People often forget about me. I guess it's what comes of being so small."

"Well, you must go to the ball," insisted Honesty.

"Come on, let's start making our ball gowns. I think I'll make mine of the finest white silk. What are you going to make yours from?"
"I don't think I'll make one," said Harmony. "I'm sure the silk worms will be busy enough spinning silk for you and the other fairies. There's no point in making them spin silk for a gown that won't be worn."

Everyone was so busy getting ready for the ball that the day it was to be held soon arrived.

Up at the palace, the Fairy Queen looked around to make sure that everything was ready. "Perfect, perfect, perfect," she sang, as she checked off things on her list. But just as she was about to put a check beside 'statues', she stopped and did a double take. The statues had disappeared. And it wasn't only the statues that had vanished. Some of her best plants and ornamental lamps had also disappeared.

Tutting loudly to herself, the Fairy Queen twirled her golden wand through the air and began to chant:

"Statues, plants, lamps and things,
reappear before the ball begins."

In a puff of golden fairy dust, the statues, plants and lamps reappeared in front of the palace.

"That's better," smiled the Fairy Queen. She was just about to turn her attention to the banquet when Rosebud, her trusty handmaiden, coughed loudly.

"Ahem! Your majesty," called Rosebud. "They're gone again."

"Fiddlesticks," shouted the Queen, stamping her foot. She whirled her wand above her head and said the spell again.

"Statues, plants, lamps and things,
reappear before the ball begins."

Everything quickly appeared in a puff of golden fairy dust, only to disappear just as fast. "How very strange. I wonder what's going on. I know. I'll call Honesty. She always gets to the bottom of these mysteries," said the Queen, throwing back her head and giving a very unqueen-like shout, "HONESTY! I NEED YOU!"

"Here I am," sang a voice, and Honesty appeared at the Fairy Queen's side. The Queen quickly explained her problem and Honesty's nose began to twitch. She followed some muddy footprints across the grass and swept back a clump of ivy. Behind it was a huddle of giggling pixies. "What we have here is a pixie problem," explained Honesty, as she pulled each one out by his ear.

"Stop messing around at once," demanded Honesty. But of course the pixies, being pixies, just giggled louder and made more things disappear. They thought it was a brilliant joke. The Fairy Queen shook her head sadly. She knew that trying to stop pixie mischief was almost always impossible.

"Stop or I'll banish you from the kingdom," she shouted. But that just made the pixies giggle louder and make more and more things disappear.

The Fairy Queen was very upset. How could she possibly throw a palace-warming ball when it didn't look its very best? "At this rate, there'll be nothing left. I think we'd better call Harmony. She'll know what to do," said Honesty. "HARMONY!"

Harmony appeared in a tiny puff of silver smoke. As soon as the problem was explained to her, Harmony knew exactly what to do. She was the peace fairy, after all. "If you invited the pixies to your ball they might just stop playing their silly tricks," she suggested to the Queen.

The Fairy Queen thought it was a wonderful idea and invited the
pixies at once. "You can only come if you stop playing tricks," she told them,
waving her finger sternly. The naughty pixies were so pleased to be invited
that they made all the decorations reappear in a flash.

In fact, they were so delighted that they even added a few things of their own. The Queen was particularly pleased with their fountain. Now the palace looked just perfect, the ball could go ahead as planned.

The Fairy Queen turned to Harmony and smiled. "To thank you for your help, I would like you to be my special guest at the ball. Give me your invitation and I'll put my royal kiss on it so everyone will know that you are to be treated like a fairy princess." Harmony blushed.
"I didn't receive an invitation," she explained

"What?" gasped the Fairy Queen. "One should have landed on your pillow ages ago. Somebody must have taken it. Somebody who likes to play tricks." She looked around and spotted the pixies trying to sneak off into the woods. "PIXIES!" she yelled. "Do you know anything about Harmony's missing invitation?"

The tallest pixie looked uncomfortable, then reached inside his pocket and pulled out an invitation addressed to Harmony. "Sorry," he muttered, as he handed it to the little fairy.

Harmony was so excited that she flapped her wings and spun in the air. "Thank you, thank you, thank you," she said to the Queen, the pixie and anyone else who would listen. She was still spinning in circles when she and Honesty arrived back at her little cottage in the woods. Then, all of a sudden, she remembered something and fell to the ground with a bump. "What's wrong?" asked Honesty, as she helped her friend to her feet.

"Oh no," cried Harmony. "I can't go to the ball, after all. I don't have a gown to wear."

"Oh, we'll soon take care of that," laughed Honesty. She pushed Harmony out the door and told her not to come back until it was time to get ready for the ball. Then she gave a high-pitched whistle and Harmony's little cottage was filled with laughing pixies. Honesty had decided that since they had taken Harmony's invitation in the first place it was only right that they made sure she went to the ball. As everyone knows, pixies are excellent dressmakers. Soon they were hard at work making a fabulous ball gown for Harmony.

That night everyone in Fairyland gathered at the new palace for the Fairy Queen's magnificent ball. The palace was decorated with shiny balloons, pretty flowers, statues, plants and of course, the pixie fountain.

Like all the other fairies, Harmony danced until dawn and had a wonderful time. She even danced with the naughty pixies, who were on their best behaviour for once!

"Goodbye, see you soon!"